THE BALL OF FIRE

FICTION WORLD

M. PAVITHRRA SRI

ISBN 979-888546132-0

This story is Dedicated to all the worm who dreams to become a butterfly. This story is also dedicated to butterflies who dreams to fly high over the sky. Lets begin !

Contents

Foreword

Hi! I Am Pavithrra Sri. MJ of 14 years , studying 9th standard have an intret in writing short stories . I also have intrest in writting quotes and I have wrote more than 100 quotes . My intrest in writting from the young age grown up with poems , stories and quotes . Which becme an hobby . Apart from writting I am also involved in drawing and listening to music . My love toward writing is combined as a book .

ONE

THE START

I am, I can , I will, I must. I am reciting this slogan in my heart, before a minute for my first match . I am proud as well. Suddenly I heard a noise "Tok Tok! ", The door open and a zombie voice keeps on increasing. It says that Megna it's already time, Hurry up! For your classes. I wonder it was a dream and the voice I heard was my mother. She again shout that Is my ears locked ? wake up, have tea, pack your bags and she left the room.

SUNSET FROM ROOM

I woke up fresh up myself and ready for my class. Once I reached there my teacher asked me that why was I late and if this repeat my internal marks will be reduced. With a sorrow face I seated . I wish the dream would come true and I will make it happen. A few years later , In a inky night the millions of rain drops patter on a man's umbrella. He hasten towards the hospital and cherished for a cry. Once he reached there, he hear a cry of his wife. The doctors were furore and tensed , he went asking for his wife. The doctor said that his wife was unable to bare the pain. Either the child or the mother would be no more. The man with shedding tears sat on the chair but closing his eyes. A huge cry flourished his ears and he was happy seeing his daughter. He named his daughter Megna Santhosh . The doctor surprised and said that it was a miracle mas by your child. Due to the nonstop kicking of the child, mother lost her energy but she manage to save her child. At last a magical theory involved and made-up the birth successful. The doctor with a grin said that she may become a footballer and he was proud to say his son is also interest in football. The man was the happiest one and now he is a responsible father to a child named Megna that's me, me.My Father Ram and My Mother Geeta is the happiest one they would say often. But then they had a worry that I was not able to walk until two years. People said that I would never walk until five years. My first step that admired the ball was at three years.

Every day I play football with my schoolmates. The ball which I kick strengthen my legs. Sometimes I would fall while kicking the ball that makes my friends to laugh at me. Saying that the ball is harder than me. While returning from school I will see brothers playing football everyday. One pleasant day , one of the brother asked me that Was I interest in playing football . I shook my head with a huge grin and I was also permitted to play. They thought me rules and restrictions to play and I literally shocked hearing it. Every day I will be the playmate and we become friends. Years passed, I need to break up my dreams to my parents . Once I exclaimed it, they said that ok but what about my studies . Since I strongly disagreed, my parents with a half heart agreed. They let me join in football academy. There I admired and inspired by my coach who was physically fit and strong in his mind. He would say that " *When mind becomes stronger situations becomes opportunity, Its all mind game* " I inspired by his words

FOOTBALL

Even though I was happy aside people would speak back that girls are unfit to play football, what if they wear a trousers in ground.The would also speak that if girls need to achieve something it must be in the four walls of kitchen and I wouldn't react to it but I think a fat comes for me and I will make it.*According to me people who speak at back push me from back , Fire us for an achievement.*

My studies went smooth but a painless rock fell on my head. My teacher calls me with my parents for a meet and I came to know the meet was to scold for my marks. In the meet, my teacher asked us that Is my books printed of football stories or any dream forms while I am writing exam every time. I just can't understand what she says. Lastly, she said that every question I wrote was personalified with the football that makes her also to laugh. Then the teacher said that may your child become a footballer with huge laugh. I was funny aside I realized that I should concentrate on my studies as well.

BOOKS

TWO
AIM AND DREAM

One pleasant day, I saw a cotton candy shop opposite of my training ground. After seeing it I forgot myself, I become a new born child and the memories strike my mind. Even I grow up I am child as heart. So I ran towards the shop .At the time I didn't notice , with my careless attitude I met with an accident. My eyes was closed

cotton candy

tightly, once I open my eyes I was able to see a different environment. Where my parents screaming to the doctor and I noticed that I couldn't lift my leg. The doctor was who treated me while I born said my mother. Since my leg is injured a lot, doctor said that I can't walk at all and I must move only with wheel chair. For my surprise the doctor son was my coach . Once I discharged from the hospital, a happy news arrived that I am selected for my first football match in India. I felt that I am standing in the top of Everest . Aside my coach forbidden me to play but I need to play that's my aim and dream. However I must walk, and I will , I will .*There is only one difference between aim and dream , Dream requires effortless sleep and Aim requires sleepless efforts Sleep for dream awake for aim.* My parents strongly disagreed for me playing in the match match. They argued that the injury may become serious and the said that if I play they wouldn't speak with me. Mom worried a lot , thinking of me all the time . She always use to tell girl child are precious and I am a gift for her. Without knowing to her I took my friend along with me to ground , I need to walk and run. I made all the accident as lie and I tried to lift myself from the wheel chair. I fall in the seat for several times, the pain I felt makes me adamant to stand up. If there is a play , there should be an adamant for a goal. That made me to take a step from the wheel chair and I had a great fall. I didn't mind it, finally I walked with the pain. Coach extremely shocked, and also scolded me for my crazy and adamant attitude. I realized the small mistake I did seeing the cotton candy, results in big injury and I would smile at me for running mad for a cotton candy.

One day, one of my friend Tharuneetha begam left her leg into Mud Sludge and she couldn't lift her leg at all . She shouted Help me! Help me! But no one bothered. Literally she started crying , her legs are paining a lot. I seeing her sitting on the wheel chair tried to get up slowly with the fractured leg. With a huge pain , cry and shout I slowly woke up from the chair. I couldn't bare the pain but then I walk slowly with a bended backbone. After few seconds I kneel down and my tear made a water bank. This incident made me walk gradually. After a while returning home, my friend to it was a drama by her it was just a drama that made you walk a little. I really shocked but I knew her friendship was really a true one and I felt I am lucky to have her. A loyal and true friend can't be found easily but can't be lost easier . Those days while we are at sixth, we would be the happiest one in the world. She also loves Cotton candy a lot and everyday we will have a fight, that the first one who eats the candy or sometimes last will win the game. The Yet to win guy will offer a cotton candy. Sometimes she will forgive for me because I was a slow eating person. Those days cannot be bought back .

COTTON CANDY

The Endless End

Finally the injury in my leg gradually decrease, that made a current shock for the doctor. He said that I have made miracle in my every fall, I am hard from my mind and heart that made me a fast relief.I am selected for under 16 and my first match. I am , can, I will, I must I am reciting this slogan before a minute for my first match. Suddenly I heard a noise shouting my teams name. The match was like 0 for 0 . It's was a hard time to hit a goal. At last the ball was passed to me near the goal post and while kicking it every incident strikes my mind. With a drop of tear mixed with smile I kick the ball harder and closed my eyes. I heard a huge noise it was a goal. We won the match and we! . *Problems are common to all but attitude makes difference* . A emotional and a proud moment in my life I would say. Now I am glade to buy cotton candy and grace the moment .If your dreams are strong you make it. Read to move for the next match! . But now I heard "Cluck Cluck " a huge clapping sound . I am a footballer attending a press meet this words will be told by Her if she is alive. Once she had a health issue that was know by her was unknown by all. Even she can quit her game but she didn't and that's my Mother. She have been a footballer to you all and a Mother to me who doesn't show her sadness but aa smile . This story resembles "I" instead " her or she "because she didn't let a chance to speak her half dark life. So I resemble her with "I ".Now I could see a drop in all of your eyes but a tear only express your feel not the real love which I had , stay happy . Jai hind!